3370900670 1640

The
Mississippi River

A Level Three Reader

By Cynthia Klingel and Robert B. Noyed

The
Child's
World®

On the cover...
This picture shows a barge as it moves
along the Mississippi River in Missouri.

Published by The Child's World®, Inc.
PO Box 326
Chanhassen, MN 55317-0326
800-599-READ
www.childsworld.com

Photo Credits
© 1993 A.B. Sheldon/Dembinsky Photo Assoc. Inc.: 5
© 1994 A.B. Sheldon/Dembinsky Photo Assoc. Inc.: 29
© Andre Jenny/Unicorn Stock Photos: 22
© A. Osinski/Image Finders: 25
© Dennis MacDonald/PhotoEdit: 13
© 1999 Dominique Braud/Dembinsky Photo Assoc. Inc.: 10, 18
© Hulton Getty: 26
© Jack Novak/Photri, Inc.: 14
© Kevin Horan/Tony Stone Images: cover
© Scott Berner/Photri, Inc.: 9
© 1997 Stephen Graham/Dembinsky Photo Assoc. Inc.: 17, 21
© Tom Bean/Tony Stone Images: 6
© XNR Productions, Inc.: 3

Project Coordination: Editorial Directions, Inc.
Photo Research: Alice K. Flanagan

Library of Congress Cataloging-in-Publication Data
Klingel, Cynthia Fitterer.
The Mississippi River / by Cynthia Klingel and Robert B. Noyed.
p. cm. — (Wonder books)
Includes Index.
Summary: Briefly describes the Mississippi River, what it looks like, its major tributaries,
where it flows, and its importance.
ISBN 1-56766-824-0 (lib. reinforced : alk. paper)
1. Mississippi River—Juvenile literature. [1. Mississippi River.]
I. Noyed, Robert B. II. Title. III. Wonder books (Chanhassen, Minn.)

F351 .K47   2000
977—dc21   99-057538

Do you know where the Mississippi River is? Here is a map to help you find it.

The Mississippi River is one of the most famous rivers in the world. It is located in the middle of the United States. It flows from the north to the south.

This part of the Mississippi River flows between Iowa and Wisconsin.

The Mississippi River is 2,552 miles (4,106 kilometers) long. It flows through 10 states. The river flows through Minnesota, Wisconsin, Iowa, Illinois, Missouri, Kentucky, Tennessee, Arkansas, Mississippi, and Louisiana.

This part of the Mississippi River is in Wisconsin.

The river begins in Itasca State Park in Minnesota. The start of the river is also known as its **headwaters.** The river is not very deep at the headwaters. People can walk in the water there.

These visitors are playing in the headwaters of the Mississippi River.

10

The Mississippi River gets much deeper as it travels through the 10 states. The widest part of the river is 3.5 miles (5.6 kilometers). The depth of the river ranges from 9 feet (2.8 meters) to 100 feet (30.5 meters).

From high above, it is easy to see how big the Mississippi River really is.

Other rivers empty into the Mississippi River. The Missouri River flows into the Mississippi near St. Louis. The muddy waters of the Missouri River change the color of the Mississippi.

This picture shows the Mississippi River's muddy waters near St. Louis, Missouri.

The Ohio River also flows into the Mississippi River. The Ohio River is large. Where the two rivers join, the Mississippi doubles in size. This spot also divides the river into the Upper Mississippi and the Lower Mississippi.

This picture shows where the Ohio and Mississippi Rivers join.

The river continues to flow south. It ends in the state of Louisiana. Just south of New Orleans, the Mississippi River empties into the Gulf of Mexico.

Here we can see many boats on the Mississippi River in New Orleans, Louisiana.

The name of the river comes from the Ojibwa Indians. The Ojibwa called the river *Mezzi-sippi*. This word means "great river." The river came to be known as the Mississippi River.

This part of the Mississippi River is in southern Minnesota.

The Mississippi River has played many important roles in the history of the United States. The river is used for shipping. **Tugboats** push large **barges** on the Mississippi.

This tugboat is pushing a long barge under a bridge on the Mississippi River.

The barges carry many things up and down the river. They often carry corn, soybeans, wheat, coal, or steel. These barges move very slowly.

 This big barge is on Iowa's part of the Mississippi River.

There are many kinds of animals along the Mississippi. The most common are **mink, muskrats, opossums,** otters, and skunks. There are also many fish in the river.

American river otters like this one →
live along the Mississippi River.

Mark Twain wrote about the Mississippi River. He is a famous writer. He worked for many years on Mississippi **riverboats.** People all over the world have learned about the river from his stories.

Here Mark Twain sits quietly to get his picture taken.

The Mississippi River is an important part of the United States. It is used to ship many things from place to place. Floating down the river is a beautiful way to travel, too.

This fancy riverboat is sailing on the Mississippi River in Wisconsin.

Glossary

barges (BAR-jez)
Barges are long, flat boats used on rivers and canals.

headwaters (HED-wah-terz)
The sources of a stream or river are called its headwaters.

mink (MINK)
Mink are small, furry animals often raised for their hides, or pelts.

muskrats (MUSK-rats)
Muskrats are small animals with webbed feet that live in and near the water.

opossums (uh-PAH-sumz)
Opossums are gray, furry animals that carry their babies in a pouch.

riverboats (RIH-ver-bohts)
Riverboats are boats for use on a river.

tugboats (TUG-bohts)
Tugboats are small, powerful boats that pull or push ships and barges.

Index

To Find Out More

Books

Baker, Sanna Anderson, and Bill Farnsworth (illustrator). *Mississippi Going North.* Morton Grove, Ill.: Albert Whitman, 1996.

Fowler, Allan. *The Mississippi River.* Danbury, Conn.: Children's Press, 1999.

Harness, Cheryl. *Mark Twain and the Queens of the Mississippi.* New York: Simon & Schuster Children's, 1998.

Twain, Mark, and Raymond Burns (illustrator). *The Adventures of Huckleberry Finn.* Mahwah, N.J.: Troll Communications, 1990.

Web Sites

The Mississippi River Headwaters Home Page
http://www.mhbriverwatch.dst.mn.us/
For information about the protection of the Mississippi River and a map of the river basin headwaters.

The Mississippi River Home Page
http://www.greatriver.com/
For information about the plants, wildlife, and history of the Mississippi River.

Note to Parents and Educators

Welcome to The Wonders of Reading™! These books provide text at three different levels for beginning readers to practice and strengthen their reading skills. Additionally, the use of nonfiction text provides readers the valuable opportunity to *read to learn*, not just to learn to read.

These leveled readers allow children to choose books at their level of reading confidence and performance. Level One books offer beginning readers simple language, word choice, and sentence structure as well as a word list. Level Two books feature slightly more difficult vocabulary, longer sentences, and longer total text. In the back of each Level Two book are an index and a list of books and Web sites for finding out more information. Level Three books continue to extend word choice and length of text. In the back of each Level Three book are a glossary, an index, and a list of books and Web sites for further research.

State and national standards in reading and language arts emphasize using nonfiction at all levels of reading development. The Wonders of Reading™ fill the historical void in nonfiction material for the primary grade readers with the additional benefit of a leveled text.

About the Authors

Cindy Klingel has worked as a high school English teacher and an elementary teacher. She is currently the curriculum director for a Minnesota school district. Writing children's books is another way for her to continue her passion for sharing the written word with children. Cindy Klingel is a frequent visitor to the children's section of bookstores and enjoys spending time with her many friends, family, and two daughters.

Bob Noyed started his career as a newspaper reporter. Since then, he has worked in communications and public relations for more than fourteen years for a Minnesota school district. He enjoys writing books for children and finds that it brings a different feeling of challenge and accomplishment from other writing projects. He is an avid reader who also enjoys music, theater, traveling, and spending time with his wife, son, and daughter.